Juma on Safari

by Lisa Maria Burgess

illustrated by Abdul M. Gugu

BARRANCA PRESS

Hello. My name is Juma. I am Tanzanian. My *Baba* is from the island of Zanzibar and my *Mama* is from the mainland of Tanzania. Like a little rabbit, I am super quick and full of tricks, so my parents call me *Super Sungura*. But most of the time, I am just Juma—Ijumaa when *Mama* wants to be serious.

Guess what? I like traveling.

My sister Sareeya and I get to visit *Bibi* for the April holiday. Our Granny lives near Seronera. That is soooooo far away from Dar es Salaam that *Mama* says we'll take two hundred naps to get there.

So we pack our bags in *Baba*'s old Corolla and go to bed early so we can get up early.

We wake up way before the sun. *Baba* drives fast on the big, big road. Soon, the sun shines on top of the trees.

Sareeya and I see coconuts and bananas and rice and maize and sisal and oranges and little villages on the side of the road. When we are tired of looking, we sleep.

We are both awake when we cross the Wami River—down, down, *pole, pole*, and up, up, *pole, pole*. In Segera, we stop to water the car and eat oranges.

Baba is driving fast again when *Mama* shouts, "There she is!" *Baba* says something that we're not supposed to hear and Sareeya asks, "Who, who, who?"

"The Queen of Africa, Mama Kilimanjaro," says *Mama*. "Usually she hides her face, but today she is peaking through the clouds at you. She is asking, "Who are these sweet children coming to greet me?"

We wave and shout so that Mama Kilimanjaro hears our greetings.

Then she hides her face and we go back to sleep. *Baba*'s old Corolla isn't so fast. It's taking more than 200 naps to reach *Bibi*'s house!

*B*aba drives through the cities of Moshi and Arusha.

Baba says too much traffic —No stopping for snacks. But every time he buys more petrol for that old Corolla, we get to run quick, quick to the toilets.

Then we are on a straight road with flat, flat land.

Sareeya and I look for goats and cattle. Each time we find them, we find Maasai herders with their walking sticks. Their villages are far away. It must take them two plus twenty plus two hundred steps to get there. I am good at mathematics.

We sleep again. When we wake, the old Corolla is groaning. The big straight road has turned into a little S-shaped road, getting lost among the trees. *Mama* says we are driving up the Ngorongoro Crater—that's a long word for a big hill with an empty middle. At the top, we look down into a giant bowl that *Mama* says was a volcano long ago. *Mama* teaches geography—can't you tell?

Suddenly, *Baba* stops. Sareeya and I fall out of our seats and hit our heads. I wish we had kept our seat belts on! We crawl back up and see the biggest, biggest elephant in the middle of the road. "Look at his tusks!" whispers *Baba*.

Guess what? I stick my head out the window and say, "*Hujambo* Mr. *Tembo*."

Guess what, what? Sareeya opens her door and walks to greet the elephant. *Mama* has to think quickly and grabs her by the dress and pulls her back in the car.

Soon, the elephant crosses to a clearing.

Baba drives up, up and down, down toward the Serengeti Plains, which is a long word for a big, flat land. Before we get there, the old Corolla decides to rest. The sun is also getting tired, so the animals are eating their last bit of grass.

Sareeya wants to count the babies—one baby zebra, three baby wildebeest, four baby gazelle…. But the baby warthogs are so fast, they are hard to count. Those little *ngiri* run crazy with their tails straight in the air.

Guess what? That *Little Sungura* thinks babies only eat flowers—white flowers, blue flowers, purple flowers….

Guess what, what? I know they only drink milk.

Mama calls my uncle on her cell phone. He leaves the lodge where he works and drives his old Land Rover to help.

When *Mjomba* arrives, he and *Baba* decide to fix the engine in the daylight.

Guess what? That is the best, best plan.

My *Mjomba* is full of stories: Once he put a dart in a lion so the game wardens could put on a tracking collar. The lion snored so much it didn't notice when *Mjomba* fell asleep on its stomach!

Another time, he took care of a cheetah whose parents were killed by poachers. That cheetah ran faster than his old Land Rover!

I will be a game warden when I get big—for sure!

Baba and *Mjomba* stretch their legs, rub their eyes, and open the bonnet again. *Mjomba* pours half the box of tea into the radiator. *Baba* adds water. The plan is for the tea leaves to stop up the holes in the radiator.

Sareeya and I bring cups of *chai ya maziwa* for their breakfast. *Baba* and *Mjomba* drink their tea.

They wait to see what that leaky old engine decides to do with its own tea. *Mjomba* says, "The trick is to give a car a good breakfast every day."

I want to know how that old Corolla is going to eat *chapati* with its tea.

On the road, there is a big pile of elephant poop. Sareeya wants to touch it. I say, "No." But it doesn't really smell bad. It just looks like a pile of muddy straw.

There is a dung beetle rolling a ball of poop. Another beetle walks over and tries to take it away. The dung beetles start a wrestling match. All their little legs wriggle as they roll onto their backs.

While they are fighting, another beetle walks over and quickly rolls that ball of poop away, far away. When the two beetles stop fighting, they turn in circles looking for that ball of poop.

Finally those silly *wadudu* understand there is nothing to fight over. They must make their own dung balls. Sareeya wants to help them, but Mama calls us back in the car.

Guess what? That old Corolla is fixed!

Guess what, what? We drive some more and some more.

Sareeya and I count baby animals: one, two, three, seven, fourteen, twenty... Finally, *Mama* says, "This is it – our little village."

I don't know if *Bibi* hears that old Corolla moaning or *Mjomba*'s old Land Rover growling, but she is at the door to greet us. She looks so happy to see us.

But she can't be as happy as we are to see her!

Tanzania

Juma lives in Dar es Salaam in the east African country of Tanzania.

Tanzania stretches east to the beaches of the Zanzibar islands, west to the plains of the mainland, south to Lake Tanganyika, and north to Lake Victoria and the peak of Mount Kilimanjaro.

People in his family speak ki-Swahili and English, as well as ki-Sukuma and other languages. Juma likes to repeat words, which is a habit in ki-Swahili: In English we might say something like "very slow", but in ki-Swahili we would say *pole, pole* ("slow, slow").

Tanzania is famous for all sorts of wonderful things – the spices grown in Zanzibar, the coffee and tea grown in the highlands and the cotton in the lowlands, the purple, blue stone called Tanzanite found deep in the earth, and of course the wild animals that live in the national parks.

AFRICA

Tanzania

Atlantic
Ocean

Indian
Ocean

Travel Route

Juma's family drives on the main highway from Dar es Salaam on the Indian Ocean.

At the town of Chalinze, they turn north.

They cross the River Wami and pass the town of Segera, Mount Kilimanjaro, the cities of Moshi and Arusha, the Ngorongoro Crater, and Olduvai Gorge.

Finally, on the Serengeti Plains, they come to a village near the town of Seronera, where Juma's grandmother lives.

Ki-Swahili and English Glossary:

Baba:	Father
Bibi:	Grandmother
Chai ya maziwa:	Tea with spices cooked in milk
Chapati:	Flat breads (like Mexican tortillas)
Hujambo:	Hello
Mama:	Mother
Mjomba:	Uncle
Pole, pole:	Slowly, slowly (carefully)
Safari:	Long journey

Animals:

Duma:	Cheetah
Fisi:	Spotted hyena
Gazella granti:	Grant's gazelle
Gazella thomsoni:	Thomson's gazelle
Wadudu:	Beetles or insects
Ngiri:	Warthog
Nyati:	African buffalo
Nyumbu:	Blue wildebeest
Punda Milia:	Zebra
Simba:	Lion
Sungura:	Rabbit
Tembo:	Elephant
Twiga:	Giraffe

About the Authors:

At the time of writing these stories, **Lisa Maria Burgess** taught in the Department of Literature at the University of Dar es Salaam. She wrote the Juma stories with her sons, **Matoko** and **Senafa**.

About the Illustrator:

Abdul M. Gugu lives in Dar es Salaam where he works as an illustrator of children's books and as an artist.

FIRST EDITION, July 2013

ISBN 978-1-939604-03-3

Library of Congress Catalog Card Number: 2013937631

Manufactured in the United States of America.

CPSIA information can be obtained at www.ICGtesting.com
Printed in the USA
LVOW020738050713

341496LV00001B/3/P